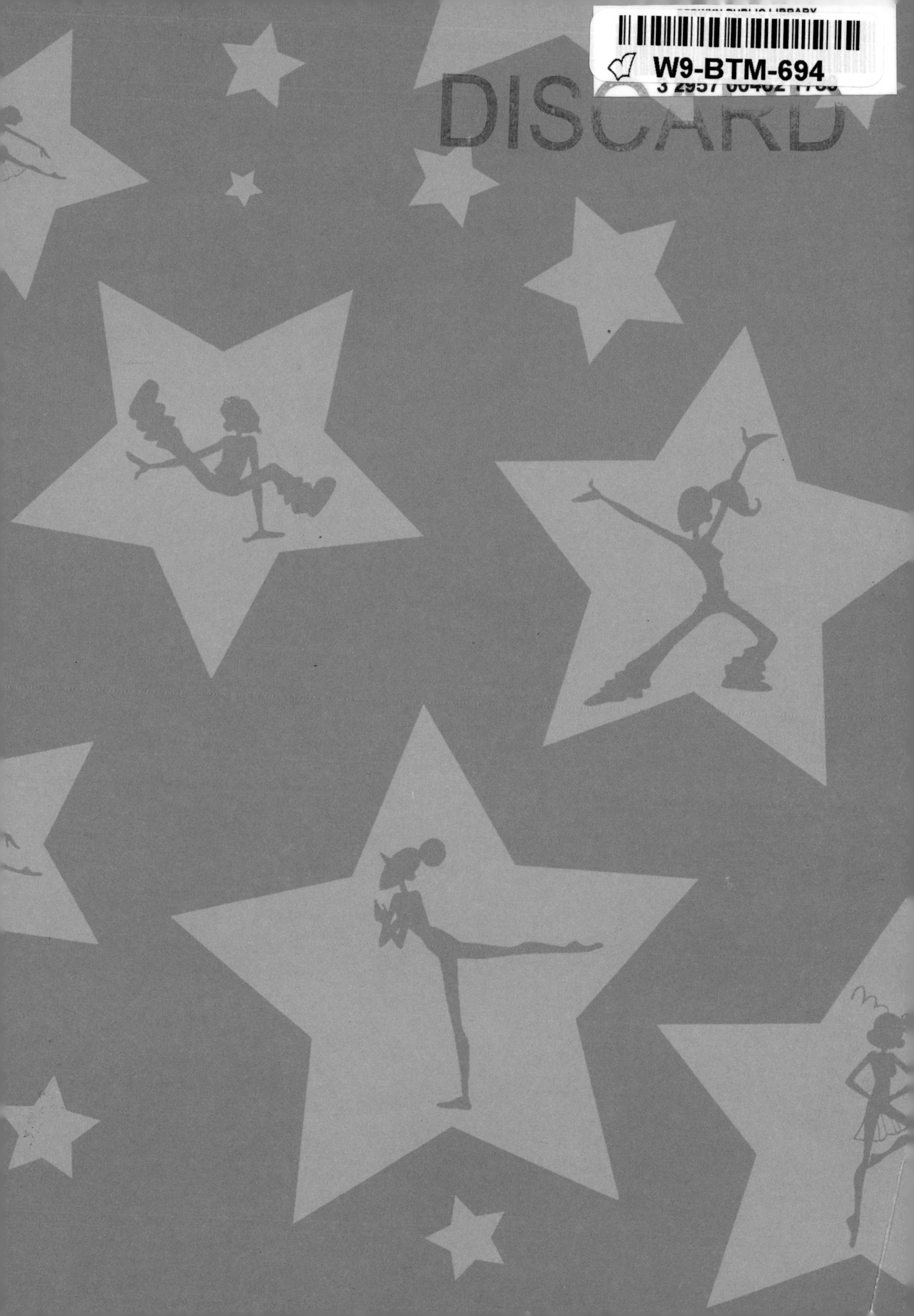

Dance Class

Crip • Art
Béka • Story
Maëla Cosson • Color

PAPERCUTZ™
New York

Dance Class Graphic Novels Available from PAPERCUTZ

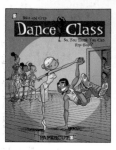

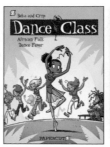

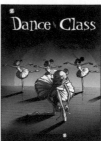

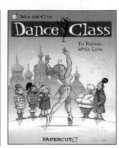

#1 "So, You Think You Can Hip-Hop?"

#2 "Romeos and Juliet"

#3 "African Folk Dance Fever"

#4 "A Funny Thing Happened on the Way to Paris..."

#5 "To Russia, With Love"

COMING SOON!

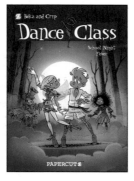

#6 "A Merry Olde Christmas"

#7 "School Night Fever"

DANCE CLASS graphic novels are available for $10.99 only in hardcover. Available from booksellers everywhere. You can also order online from Papercutz.com. Or call 1-800-886-1223, Monday through Friday, 9 - 5 EST. MC, Visa, and AmEx accepted. To order by mail, please add $4.00 for postage and handling for first book ordered, $1.00 for each additional book and make check payable to NBM Publishing. Send to: Papercutz, 160 Broadway, Suite 700, East Wing, New York, NY 10038.

DANCE CLASS graphic novels are also available digitally wherever e-books are sold.

Papercutz.com

Dance Class

Studio Danse [Dance Class], by Béka & Crip
© 2012 BAMBOO ÉDITION.
www.bamboo.fr
All other editorial material © 2013 by Papercutz.

DANCE CLASS #6
A Merry Olde Christmas"

Béka - writer
Crip - Artist
Maëla Cosson - Colorist
Joe Johnson - Translation
Tom Orzechowski - Lettering
Beth Scorzato - Production Coordinator
Michael Petranek - Editor
Jim Salicrup
Editor-in-Chief

ISBN: 978-1-59707-442-1

Printed in China
September 2013 by New Era Printing LTD.
Unit C, 8/F Worldwide Centre
123 Chung Tau, Kowloon, Hong Kong

Papercutz books may be purchased for business or promotional use. For information on bulk purchases please contact Macmillan Corporate and Premium Sales Department at (800) 221-7945 x5442.

Distributed by Macmillan
First Papercutz Printing

SOME DAYS SEEM LIKE ALL THE OTHERS...

...BUT APPEARANCES CAN BE DECEIVING.

IN FACT, TODAY IS A SPECIAL DAY...

...FOR A GREAT BIT OF NEWS AWAITS US.

NOTHING SEEMS ANY DIFFERENT THIS DAY...

UNTIL THE DAY IS ALMOST DONE...

?

OH! A LETTER FROM PRUNE!

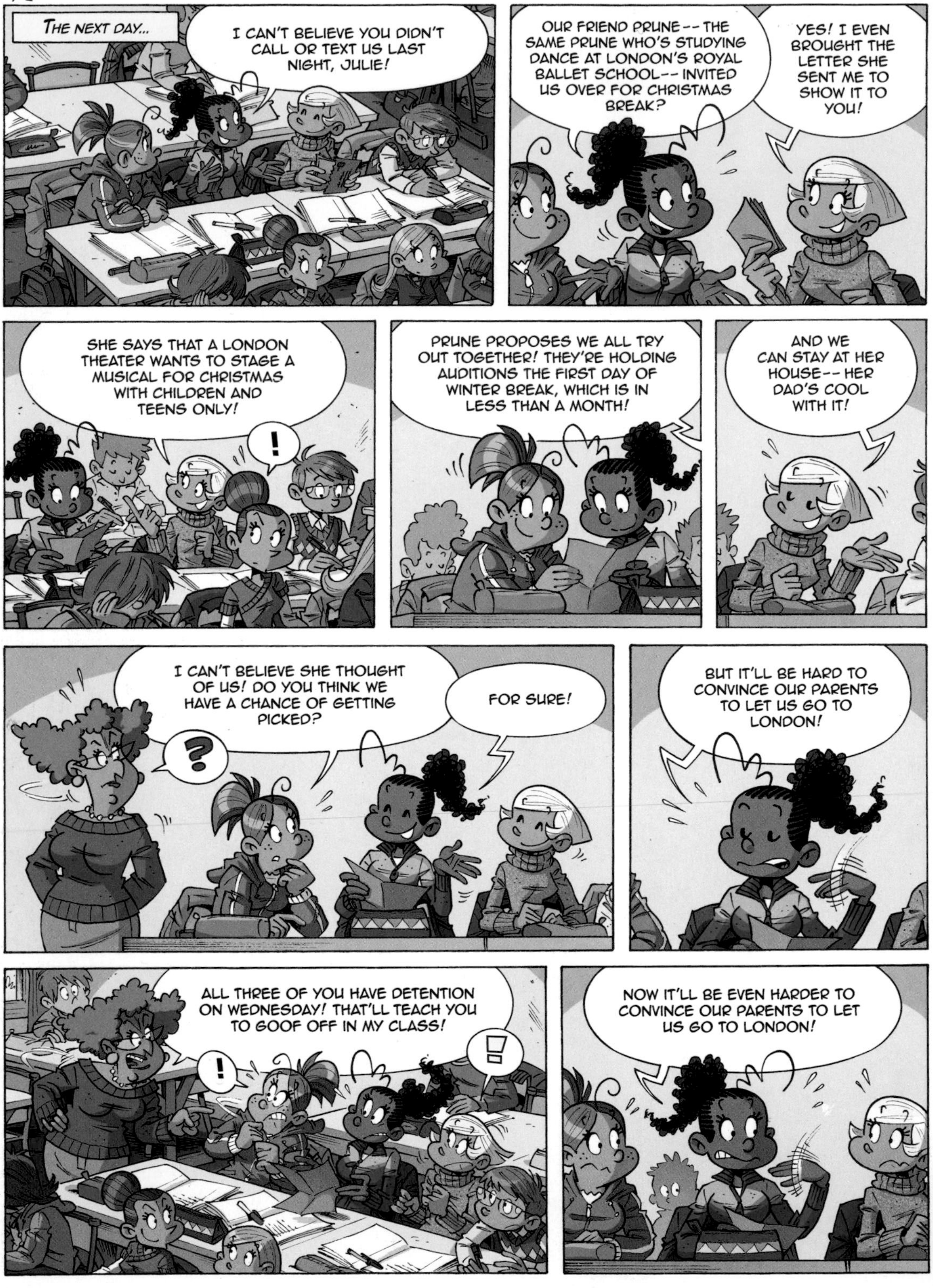
THE NEXT DAY...
I CAN'T BELIEVE YOU DIDN'T CALL OR TEXT US LAST NIGHT, JULIE!
OUR FRIEND PRUNE-- THE SAME PRUNE WHO'S STUDYING DANCE AT LONDON'S ROYAL BALLET SCHOOL-- INVITED US OVER FOR CHRISTMAS BREAK?
YES! I EVEN BROUGHT THE LETTER SHE SENT ME TO SHOW IT TO YOU!
SHE SAYS THAT A LONDON THEATER WANTS TO STAGE A MUSICAL FOR CHRISTMAS WITH CHILDREN AND TEENS ONLY!
!
PRUNE PROPOSES WE ALL TRY OUT TOGETHER! THEY'RE HOLDING AUDITIONS THE FIRST DAY OF WINTER BREAK, WHICH IS IN LESS THAN A MONTH!
AND WE CAN STAY AT HER HOUSE-- HER DAD'S COOL WITH IT!
I CAN'T BELIEVE SHE THOUGHT OF US! DO YOU THINK WE HAVE A CHANCE OF GETTING PICKED?
FOR SURE!
?
BUT IT'LL BE HARD TO CONVINCE OUR PARENTS TO LET US GO TO LONDON!
ALL THREE OF YOU HAVE DETENTION ON WEDNESDAY! THAT'LL TEACH YOU TO GOOF OFF IN MY CLASS!
!
!
NOW IT'LL BE EVEN HARDER TO CONVINCE OUR PARENTS TO LET US GO TO LONDON!

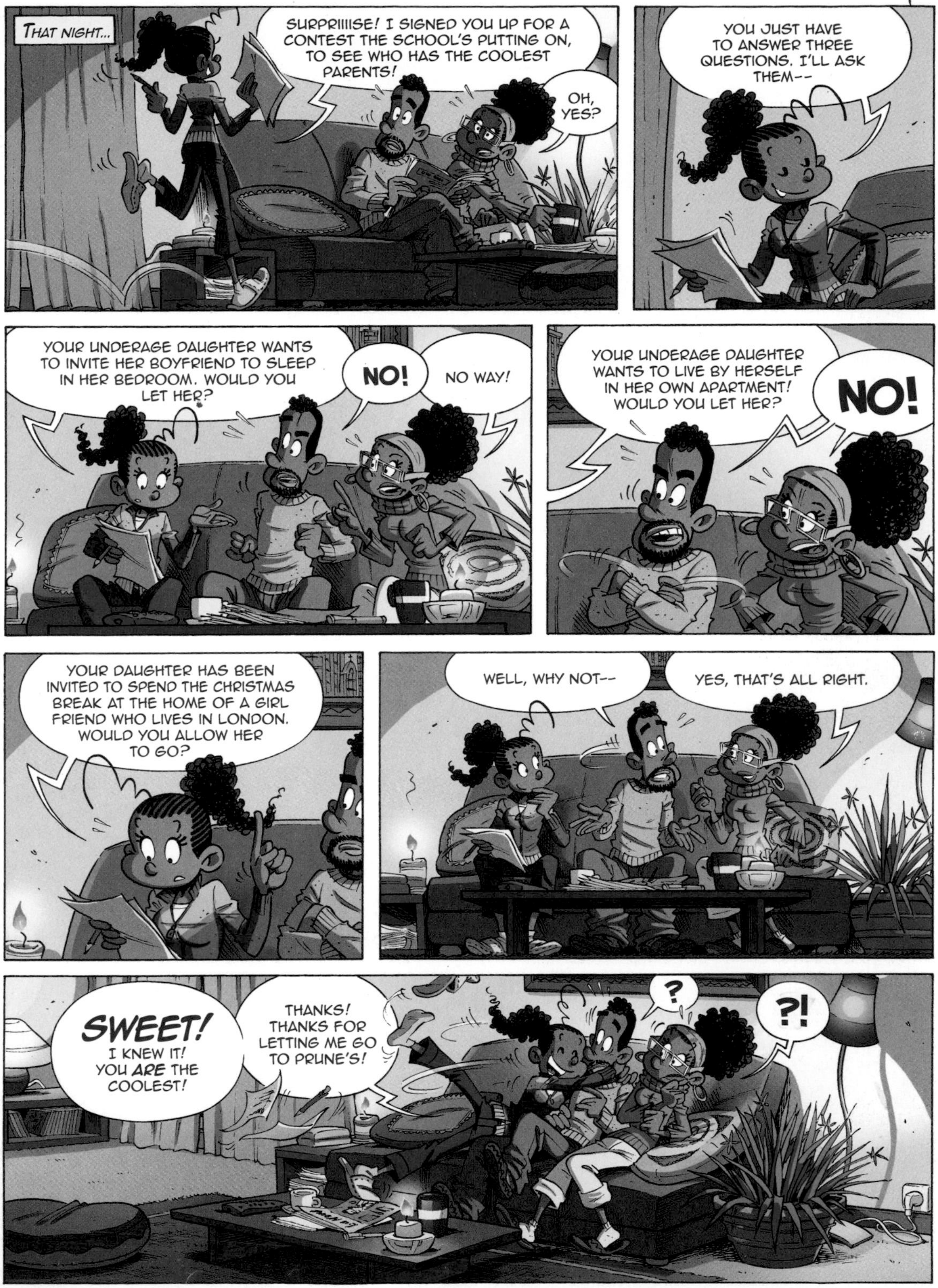
THAT NIGHT...
SURPRIIIISE! I SIGNED YOU UP FOR A CONTEST THE SCHOOL'S PUTTING ON, TO SEE WHO HAS THE COOLEST PARENTS!
OH, YES?
YOU JUST HAVE TO ANSWER THREE QUESTIONS. I'LL ASK THEM--
YOUR UNDERAGE DAUGHTER WANTS TO INVITE HER BOYFRIEND TO SLEEP IN HER BEDROOM. WOULD YOU LET HER?
NO!
NO WAY!
YOUR UNDERAGE DAUGHTER WANTS TO LIVE BY HERSELF IN HER OWN APARTMENT! WOULD YOU LET HER?
NO!
YOUR DAUGHTER HAS BEEN INVITED TO SPEND THE CHRISTMAS BREAK AT THE HOME OF A GIRL FRIEND WHO LIVES IN LONDON. WOULD YOU ALLOW HER TO GO?
WELL, WHY NOT--
YES, THAT'S ALL RIGHT.
SWEET! I KNEW IT! YOU ARE THE COOLEST!
THANKS! THANKS FOR LETTING ME GO TO PRUNE'S!
?
?!

I'VE BROUGHT YOU TOGETHER BECAUSE CHRISTMAS IS COMING AND, LIKE EVERY YEAR SINCE YOUR DIVORCE, THERE'LL BE A PROBLEM...

DAD WILL WANT ME TO SPEND THE HOLIDAYS WITH HIM, MOM WITH HER, AND YOU'LL HAVE ANOTHER ARGUMENT!

THERE'S NO PROBLEM! SINCE YOU WERE AT YOUR DAD'S LAST YEAR, YOU'LL BE WITH ME THIS YEAR!

LUCIE WAS WITH ME ON THE 25th! BUT I'LL REMIND YOU THAT YOU PICKED HER UP ON THE 26th AT DAWN AND KEPT HER THE WHOLE REST OF THE BREAK!

MAYBE! BUT YOU GOT HER *1 DAY EXTRA* AT EASTER AND--

STOP!

I'LL GET YOU TO AGREE. I WON'T GO TO DAD'S--

HA!

!

--BUT I WON'T GO TO MOM'S, EITHER!

HUH?

I'LL GO TO PRUNE'S. SHE'S INVITED ME TO LONDON FOR THE CHRISTMAS BREAK, ALONG WITH JULIE AND ALIA!

THAT'S NICE, EH? THANKS TO HER, OUR PROBLEMS ARE SOLVED!

!

⇒MMMM⇐... THIS CRÊPE IS DELICIOUS!

!

YUM YUM!

IT'S A CATASTROPHE!

?
?

MY ENGLISH GRADE IS FALLING! LOOK AT MY LAST HOMEWORK ASSIGNMENT!

BUT YOU GOT A B+!

YES! BUT BEFORE, I HAD AN A! DON'T YOU SEE?

IT'S THE BEGINNING OF THE END! WHERE WILL IT STOP?!

?!
!

I THINK I MUST TAKE RADICAL STEPS!

SO WHAT IF I WENT TO PRACTICE MY ENGLISH IN LONDON DURING THE CHRISTMAS BREAK?

PRUNE'S INVITED ME, IN FACT...

!

?!

THE NEXT DAY...

WELL?

IT WORKED!

FOR ME, TOO!

THREE WEEKS LATER, IN LONDON...

PRUNE! WE'RE HERE!

eurostar

YOU DIDN'T HAVE TO WAIT FOR US ON THE STATION PLATFORM!

I COULDN'T WAIT TO SEE YOU AGAIN, GIRLS!

ARE YOU ALL DOING WELL?

GREAT! EXCEPT ALIA, WHO'S A LITTLE POUTY...

IT'S BECAUSE WE MADE HER LIMIT HERSELF TO ONE SUITCASE. AT FIRST, SHE WANTED TO BRING HER WHOLE WARDROBE.

IF I BLOW THE AUDITION BECAUSE I DON'T HAVE THE RIGHT OUTFIT, I'LL NEVER SPEAK TO YOU AGAIN!

YOU KNOW, ALIA, IT'S BETTER TO TRAVEL LIGHT. ESPECIALLY SINCE WE HAVE TO TAKE THE SUBWAY AND, AT THIS HOUR, IT'S CROWDED!

?

OOOH! AMERICAN GIRLS! WELCOME! U-S-A! U-S-A!

HEE HEE! THAT LADY WAS FUNNY!

YES! CERTAIN ENGLISH PEOPLE ARE A LITTLE ECCENTRIC AT TIMES!

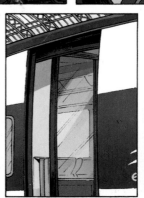

THAT'S GOOD! JULIE, LUCIE, AND ALIA DIDN'T NOTICE I WAS ON THE TRAIN!

HEH HEH! I CAN'T WAIT TO SEE THE LOOKS ON THEIR FACES TOMORROW, ONCE THEY LEARN I'VE SIGNED UP FOR THE AUDITION, TOO!

IN THE MEANTIME, I MUST FIND THAT LADY WHO'S HOSTING ME. ACCORDING TO WHAT SHE SAID TO ME ON THE PHONE, I'LL RECOGNIZE HER EASILY--

HELLO, CARLA! WELCOME TO LONDON!

!

A BIT LATER...

HOW LUCKY YOU'RE STAYING WITH ME! I HAVE TWO PASSIONS: THE U.S. AND MUSICALS!

AT PRUNE'S...

COME IN, GIRLS! MY DAD ISN'T HERE. HE ALWAYS WORKS VERY LATE.

WE'RE ALL FOUR GOING TO STAY IN MY ROOM! IT'S BIG ENOUGH FOR THAT!

AH! YOU SEE I COULD HAVE BROUGHT ONE OR TWO MORE SUITCASES!

I SUGGEST WE GO TO BED EARLY TONIGHT. THE AUDITIONS START AT 7 O'CLOCK TOMORROW MORNING.

YOU'RE RIGHT, PRUNE, WE HAVE TO BE IN TOP FORM!

AT THE SAME MOMENT...

♪TOONIIIGHT! TOONIIIGHT!

THAT'S THE THIRD MUSICAL SHE'S SUNG SINCE I GOT HERE! I HOPE IT'S THE LAST!

THE NEXT MORNING, AT THE THEATER WHERE THE AUDITIONS ARE BEING HELD...

THAT'S STRANGE! THERE AREN'T MANY PEOPLE HERE!

YES! BUT IT'S PAST 7 O'CLOCK!

!

OH, NO! MEG'S HERE...

SHE'S A NUISANCE AT MY DANCE SCHOOL! SHE'S ALWAYS PLOTTING SOME NASTY PRANK!

HEY, PRUNE! SO YOU MANAGED TO SEE THE ANNOUNCEMENT FOR THIS AUDITION IN THE ROYAL BALLET'S HALL BEFORE I TORE IT DOWN...

NOW I UNDERSTAND WHY THERE'S SO FEW OF US!

IT'S CRAZY HOW THAT GIRL REMINDS ME OF CARLA!

AH, YES! I REMEMBER CARLA! YOU COULDN'T STAND THE SIGHT OF HER! ESPECIALLY YOU, ALIA...

YOU'RE EXAGGERATING! IT'S NOT TRUE I CAN'T STAND THE SIGHT OF HER.

?

AND HELLO...

I DO SEE HER!

!

?!

CARLA?! WHAT ARE YOU DOING HERE?

I HEARD YOU TALKING AT SCHOOL ABOUT THIS AUDITION! SO I SIGNED UP FOR IT, WITH MY MOTHER'S HELP!

I CERTAINLY WASN'T GOING TO LET SUCH A NICE OPPORTUNITY TO SHOWCASE MY TALENT ON THE ENGLISH STAGE SLIP BY!

HEH HEH! I THINK I'VE SUCCEEDED AGAIN IN ELIMINATING ANOTHER COMPETITOR! I HID A BAG CONTAINING DANCE STUFF.

!

I DON'T KNOW WHO SHE IS, BUT SHE'S GOING TO HAVE TROUBLE DANCING WITHOUT HER OUTFIT! HEH HEH!

I MANAGED TO SHUT THE THEATER'S DOOR! AND I EVEN HUNG A **"CLOSED"** SIGN ON IT!

NOT BAD! YOU KNOW, THE TWO OF US COULD LAND THE LEADING ROLES IF WE WORK TOGETHER!

WHY NOT! AFTER ALL, THERE'S NOT MANY PEOPLE LEFT TO ELIMINATE!

THIS AUDITION'S PROMISING TO BE HARDER THAN PLANNED! BESIDES THE STRESS, WE'LL HAVE TO DEAL WITH **TWO CARLAS!**

LADIES, YOUR ATTENTION PLEASE!

WE'RE GETTING STARTED! FIRST, I'LL SHOW YOU A CHOREOGRAPHY, WHICH YOU MUST THEN REPRODUCE!

HOWEVER... UH... I'LL HAVE TO DANCE IN MY JEANS...

MY BAG WITH MY DANCE STUFF HAS MYSTERIOUSLY DISAPPEARED, AND I CAN'T SEEM TO FIND IT!

! **!**

SOON AFTER...

WE'LL HAVE A SHORT BREAK, THEN YOUR TURN!

AND THERE!

FIVE MINUTES LATER...

THERE'S EVEN FEWER OF US, IT SEEMS TO ME?

YES! I TOOK ADVANTAGE OF THE BREAK TO LOCK TWO OTHER GIRLS IN THE BATH-ROOM!

MUSIC!

SMAK

!

OUCH!

CRUNCH

!

STOP!

YOU TWO, THERE!

US?

I'LL TAKE YOU! YOU'LL BE PERFECT IN THE ROLE OF THE EVIL SPIRITS!

YOU OTHERS, WE'LL CONTINUE!

THAT EVENING...

TOOM TOOM TOOM

?

WHAT'S GOING ON HERE?

TOOM

DAD! WE DID IT! WE'RE GOING TO BE PART OF THE MUSICAL!

ALL FOUR OF US!

TOOM

TOOM

WAHOO!

TOOM

STILL, IT'S THANKS TO MEG AND CARLA THAT WE GOT SELECTED!

OH, YES! ONCE THEY LEFT THE STAGE, WE ALL FELT SO RELIEVED WE DANCED GREAT!

TOOM

TOOM

I WONDER IF THEY'RE CELEBRATING, TOO?

AT THE SAME TIME...

I DON'T UNDERSTAND WHY YOUR FRIEND MEG REFUSED TO STAY! WE'RE HAVING SUCH FUN!

THE NEXT DAY, AT THE THEATER...

OKAY! WE HAVE ONLY EIGHT DAYS OF REHEARSALS BEFORE THE PERFORMANCE ON DECEMBER 25th! THERE'S NOT A MOMENT TO LOSE!

THIS MUSICAL WILL BE A MODERN VERSION OF THE CHARLES DICKENS STORY: *A CHRISTMAS CAROL!*

JULIE WILL BE SPANGLE, THE SPIRIT OF THE PARTY, LUCIE WILL BE COOKIE, THE SPIRIT OF JOY, AND ALIA WILL BE MITTEN, THE SPIRIT OF SNOW.

ALL THREE OF YOU WILL TRY TO GET THE CHRISTMAS SPIRIT INTO PRUNE, A BUSINESSWOMAN WHO THINKS OF NOTHING BUT HER WORK!

BUT THE TWO EVIL SPIRITS WILL DO EVERYTHING TO STOP YOU!

CARLA WILL BE MOROSE, THE SPIRIT OF SOLITUDE, AND MEG WILL BE BLING, THE SPIRIT OF ALL EXCESSES!

AND WHO WILL YOU BE?

I'M PRUNE'S SWEETHEART!

OH...

UH... JUST IN THE SHOW...

OOH!

As the days go by, the rehearsals come one after the other...

IF ALIA COULD STOP STARING AT PRUNE'S SWEETHEART, IT'D BE A LOT BETTER!

IF PRUNE'S SWEETHEART COULD STOP STARING AT ALIA, IT'D BE A LOT BETTER!

IF THE LADY IN PINK WHO'S ATTENDING REHEARSALS COULD STOP SINGING, IT'D BE A LOT BETTER!

OH, SORRY!

HAS ANYONE SEEN ALIA AND PRUNE'S SWEETHEART?!

...Till December 25th, the day of the show's premiere.

A Christmas CAROL

YOU'LL SEE, I ALREADY KNOW ALL THE SONGS!

?!

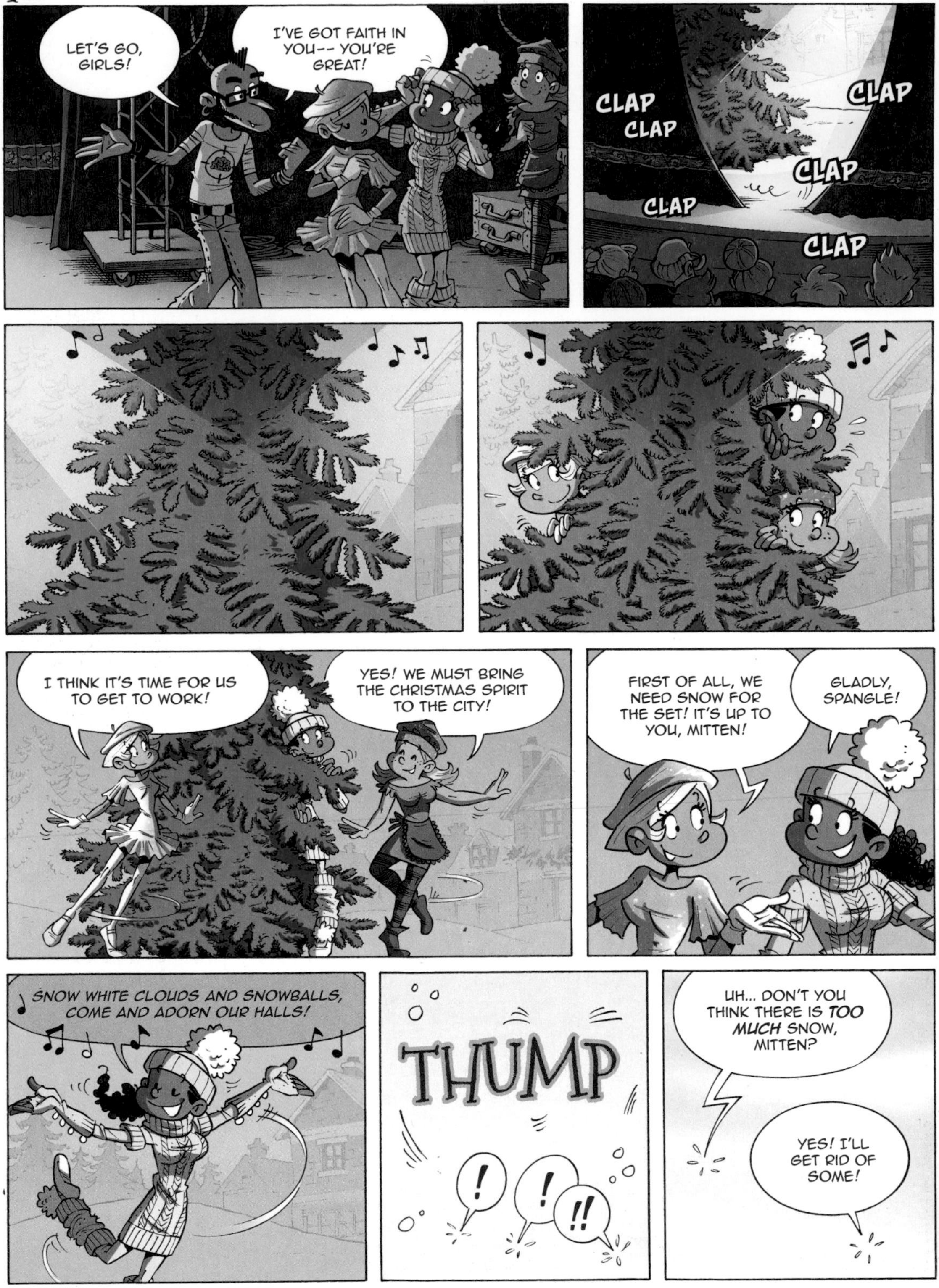
LET'S GO, GIRLS!
I'VE GOT FAITH IN YOU-- YOU'RE GREAT!
CLAP CLAP CLAP CLAP CLAP CLAP
I THINK IT'S TIME FOR US TO GET TO WORK!
YES! WE MUST BRING THE CHRISTMAS SPIRIT TO THE CITY!
FIRST OF ALL, WE NEED SNOW FOR THE SET! IT'S UP TO YOU, MITTEN!
GLADLY, SPANGLE!
SNOW WHITE CLOUDS AND SNOWBALLS, COME AND ADORN OUR HALLS!
THUMP
!
!
!!
UH... DON'T YOU THINK THERE IS TOO MUCH SNOW, MITTEN?
YES! I'LL GET RID OF SOME!

THERE, THAT'S PERFECT! NOW, IT'S OUR TURN!

AT CHRISTMAS, MAY EVERYTHING BE PRETTY...

...GIFTS AND SHOPS, THE WHOLE CITY!

NOW, FOR ONCE, DON'T RESIST YULE LOGS, NOUGATS, CANDY AND CHOCOLATE!

WHETHER YOU'RE SHORT, WHETHER YOU'RE TALL, IN THE SNOW, WE'RE KIDS ONE AND ALL!

UGH! DID YOU SEE, BLING? THE CHRISTMAS SPIRITS HAVE SUCCEEDED IN SPREADING JOY!

YES, MOROSE! IT'S TIME TO INTERVENE AND SABOTAGE THEIR WORK!

WHY ARE YOU HERE, IT'S COLD IN THE SNOW! QUICK! QUICK! TO HOME YOU MUST GO!

NOTHING'S TOO NICE, NOTHING'S TOO DEAR, BUY, OVERDO, WASTE, NEVER FEAR!

A CONFERENCE CALL ON THE 25th? I'LL BE THERE!

?

DID YOU SEE, COOKIE? THAT LADY SEEMS INDIFFERENT TO THE CHARMS OF CHRISTMAS!

YES! WE'LL HAVE TO TRY TO MAKE HER FORGET ABOUT HER JOB A LITTLE!

I HAVE AN IDEA! LET'S MAKE HER RELIVE LOVELY CHRISTMAS MOMENTS! LET'S TAKE HER BACK TO THE TIME WHEN SHE WAS A CHILD, FOR INSTANCE.

GOOD IDEA, SPANGLE!

HEH HEH! THAT ONE SEEMS TO BE WON OVER TO OUR CAUSE! SHE DOESN'T GIVE A HOOT ABOUT THE HOLIDAYS!

YES! WE'LL DO EVERYTHING TO KEEP HER!

CLAP
CLAP
CLAP
CLAP
CLAP
CLAP

WHY ARE YOU HERE, IT'S COLD IN THE SNOW! QUICK! QUICK! TO HOME YOU MUST GO!

UH... MADAM, THAT'S IT! THE FIRST ACT IS OVER!

THE SECOND ACT IS STARTING! IT'S YOUR TURN TO GO ON STAGE!

THAT'S THE LITTLE GIRL WHO'S PLAYING THE ROLE OF PRUNE AS A CHILD? SHE DOESN'T LOOK MUCH LIKE HER!

EXACTLY! SHE'S PRETTIER THAN PRUNE AND DANCES WAY BETTER!

AH! YOU'RE FINALLY AWAKE!

IT'S CHRISTMAS TODAY!

QUICK, LET'S GO AND SEE, WHAT SANTA CLAUS LEFT UNDER THE TREE!

WHAT DO ALL THESE LOVELY BOXES HOLD? THE BEAUTIFUL GIFTS OF WHICH YOU WERE TOLD!

YES, BUT TAKE A CLOSER LOOK! YOUR NAME'S ON NOTHING, NOT EVEN A BOOK!

NONE OF THE PACKAGES IS FOR YOU! NO DANCING SHOES...

WAAAH!

‑BOOHOO!‑

I'M THE ONE WHO STOLE THEM AWAY, THESE BEAUTIFUL SLIPPERS FOR BALLET!

I HATE CHRISTMAS!

⇉BOO-HOO!⇇

WE'VE FAILED!

I HAVE ANOTHER IDEA: WHAT IF WE HAD HER RELIVE A LOVELY CHRISTMAS MOMENT WITH HER FIRST SWEETHEART!

VERY GOOD! IT'S TIME TO CHANGE THE SET, AND WE'LL CONTINUE ON WITH THE FOLLOWING SCENE!

⇉BOO-HOO!⇇

CARLA! GIVE HER THE DANCE SLIPPERS! WE PROMISED HER SHE COULD KEEP THEM AFTER THE SHOW!

A FEW MOMENTS LATER...

ROASTED CHESTNUTS WARM AND CREAMY...

...PERFECT FOR LOVERS DREAMY!

WHAT IF WE HAD SOME?

WHY NOT?...

DON'T WAIT, NOW'S THE RIGHT TIME, TO SHARE WITH HER YOUR FEELINGS SUBLIME!

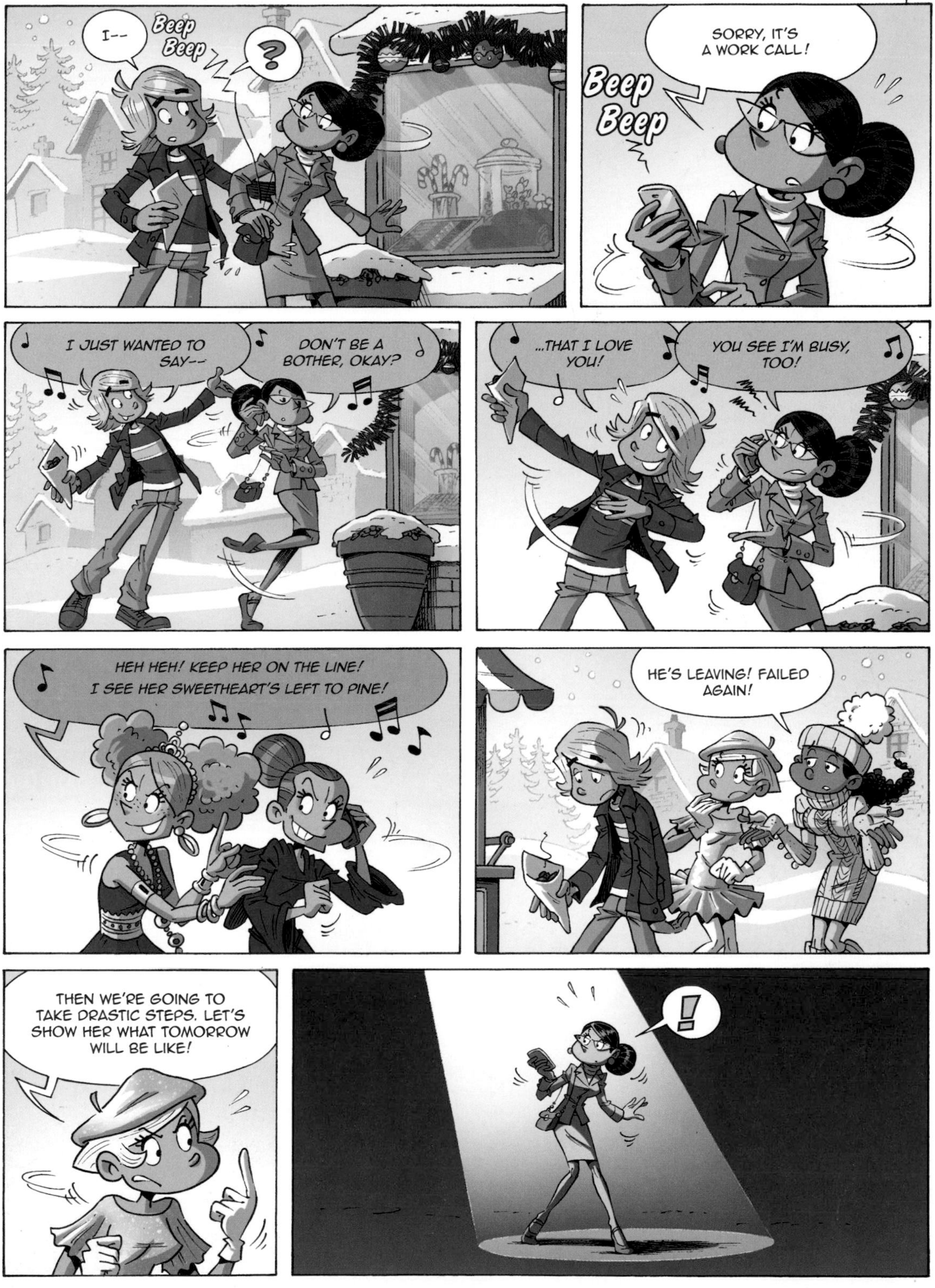
I--
Beep Beep
?
SORRY, IT'S A WORK CALL!
Beep Beep
I JUST WANTED TO SAY--
DON'T BE A BOTHER, OKAY?
...THAT I LOVE YOU!
YOU SEE I'M BUSY, TOO!
HEH HEH! KEEP HER ON THE LINE! I SEE HER SWEETHEART'S LEFT TO PINE!
HE'S LEAVING! FAILED AGAIN!
THEN WE'RE GOING TO TAKE DRASTIC STEPS. LET'S SHOW HER WHAT TOMORROW WILL BE LIKE!
!

BUT WHAT'S HAPPENING?

WHY AM I ALL ALONE IN THE DARK?

THAT'S WHAT HAPPENS TO THOSE WITHOUT FRIENDS IN WHOSE LIFE WORK ALL TRANSCENDS!

BUT! THAT'S NOT WHAT I WANTED!

HELP!

HELP ME!

IT'S EASY TO CHANGE YOUR WAYS, WE'LL GIVE YOU THE CHANCE, SEIZE THE DAY!

!

beep beep beep beep

COME! COME QUICK, MY FRIENDS!

PARTY AT MY PLACE, DON'T BE LATE! CHRISTMAS IS A TIME TO CELEBRATE!

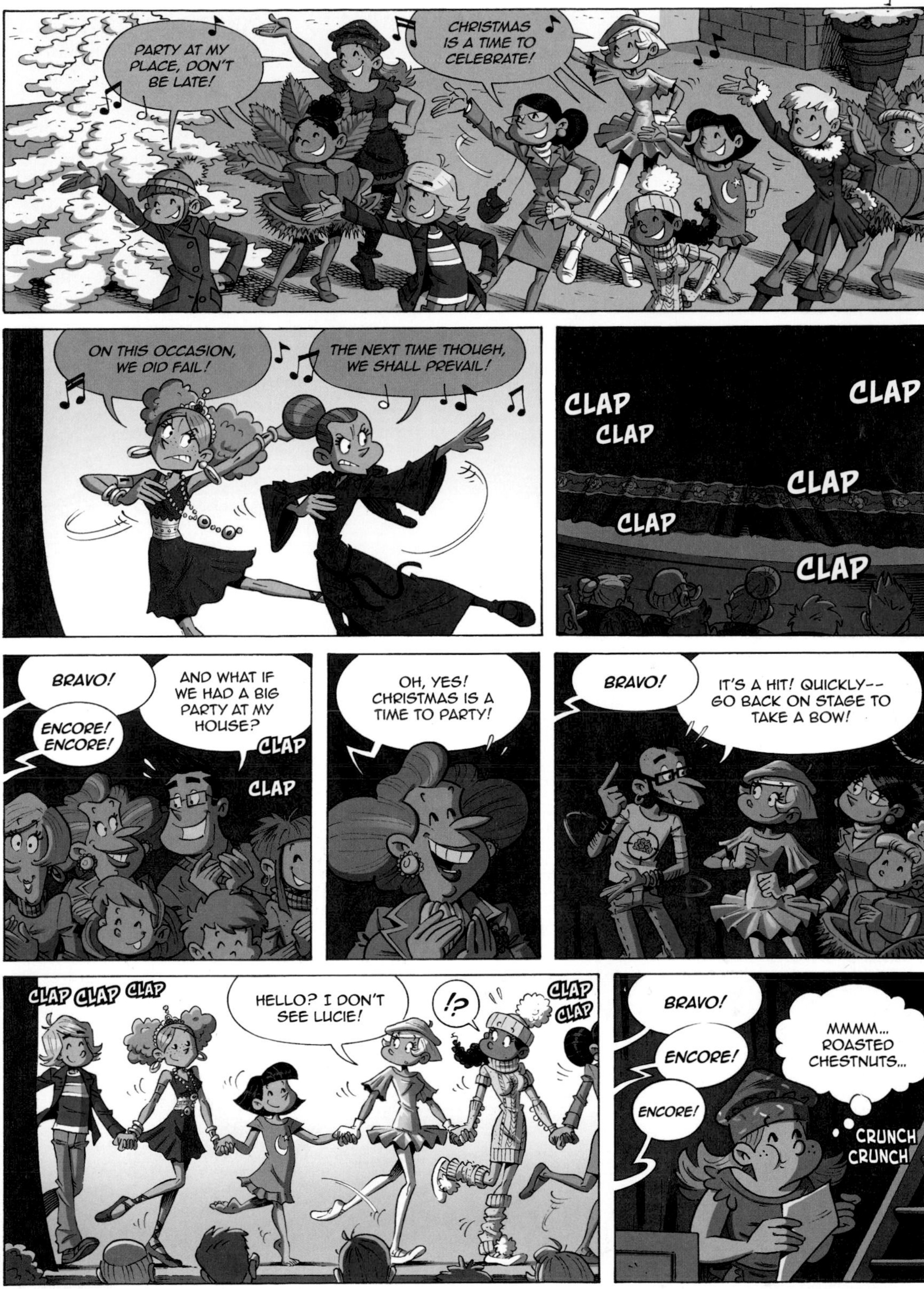
PARTY AT MY PLACE, DON'T BE LATE!
CHRISTMAS IS A TIME TO CELEBRATE!
ON THIS OCCASION, WE DID FAIL!
THE NEXT TIME THOUGH, WE SHALL PREVAIL!
CLAP
CLAP
CLAP
CLAP
CLAP
CLAP
BRAVO!
ENCORE! ENCORE!
AND WHAT IF WE HAD A BIG PARTY AT MY HOUSE?
CLAP
CLAP
OH, YES! CHRISTMAS IS A TIME TO PARTY!
BRAVO!
IT'S A HIT! QUICKLY-- GO BACK ON STAGE TO TAKE A BOW!
CLAP CLAP CLAP
HELLO? I DON'T SEE LUCIE!
!?
CLAP CLAP
BRAVO!
ENCORE!
ENCORE!
MMMM... ROASTED CHESTNUTS...
CRUNCH CRUNCH

That night, at Prune's...

OUR SHOW IS A GREAT SUCCESS!

YES! IT SEEMS THAT TICKETS FOR THE NEXT SHOWS ARE SELLING LIKE HOTCAKES!

THIS STAY IN LONDON TRULY SEEMS LIKE A DREAM!

EXCEPT MAYBE FOR ALIA!

?

OH? IS THERE A PROBLEM?

SHE'S NOT WITH HER BOYFRIEND ANYMORE! WHEN ALIA WAS ON THE PHONE, MEG WAS FLIRTING WITH HIM. THEY'VE ALREADY STARTED DATING!

CLEARLY, THAT BOY CAN'T STAND FOR GIRLS TO BE ON THE PHONE! YOU'RE NOT TOO SAD, ALIA?

OH, NO!

I FIGURED YOU CAN'T ALWAYS WIN AGAINST EVIL SPIRITS!

THE HAPPIEST ONE OF ALL OF US IS YOUR DAD, PRUNE!

YES! HEE HEE HEE!

EVER SINCE YOU GOT HERE, HE'S BECOME A FAN OF DANCE!

A FEW DAYS LATER...

IT WAS WONDERFUL, PRUNE! WE'LL NEVER FORGET THIS VACATION!

ME EITHER! ALL FOUR OF US REALLY MAKE A GREAT TEAM!

AND TO THINK I'LL BE ALL ALONE WITH MEG ONCE YOU'RE NO LONGER HERE!

EXCUSE ME!

SMACK

!

IF IT'S ANY CONSOLATION TO YOU, JUST TELL YOURSELF WE'LL BE WITH CARLA!

SEE YOU VERY SOON, PRUNE!

HAVE A GOOD TRIP BACK!

IN ANY CASE, YOU WERE RIGHT, GIRLS! IT WAS SMART NOT TO BRING TOO MUCH BAGGAGE COMING TO LONDON!

PFFF

BECAUSE WITH ALL THE THINGS I'VE BOUGHT, I'D HAVE NEVER BEEN ABLE TO CARRY EVERYTHING!

SOME DAYS SEEM LIKE ALL THE OTHERS...

ROYAL BALLET SCHOOL

RICHMOND PARK
LONDON

...BUT APPEARANCES CAN BE DECEIVING.

IN FACT, TODAY IS A SPECIAL DAY...

...FOR A GREAT BIT OF NEWS AWAITS US.

NOTHING SEEMS ANY DIFFERENT THIS DAY...

UNTIL THE DAY IS ALMOST DONE....

!

Thanks!
Your friends
for life!
Julie,
Lucie,
and Alia!

THE END

WHAT ARE YOU DOING, ALIA?

I'M LOOKING ALL AROUND ME BECAUSE WE START DOING AFRICAN DANCE AGAIN TODAY...

...AND YOU SHOULD DO THE SAME, AS MUCH AS YOU CAN!

SHORTLY AFTER...

TOO TOOM

TOOM

TOOM

LET YOURSELVES GO, GIRLS! LET IT OUT!

TOO TOOM

PERFECT! WE'LL STOP WITH THAT THIS TIME!

⸮OWW!⸮ MY NECK!

I CAN'T MOVE MY NECK NOW!

I'D TOLD YOU TO TAKE YOUR CHANCE EARLIER!

WOW! WHAT ENERGY, MARY! ARE YOU TRYING A NEW STYLE?

NO! ⇒PFFFUUH⇐

NOT AT ALL, KT!

IT'S JUST THAT THE ROOM'S RADIATOR'S BROKEN DOWN! ⇒PFUUUH⇐ SO WE'RE WARMING UP AS BEST WE CAN!

PUFF!

HUFF!

HUFF! PUFF!

HEY, GIRLS! I HAVE AN IDEA!

WHAT IF WE ORGANIZED A FLASH MOB AMONGST OURSELVES?

A WHAT?

A FLASH MOB DANCE! IT'S WHEN PEOPLE MEET UP IN A SPECIFIC LOCATION TO DANCE TOGETHER!

OH, YES, GOOD IDEA!

IT'D BE FUN!

BUT WHERE WOULD WE DO IT?

WHY NOT AT THE SQUARE?

OH, NO! IT'S TOO FAR!

IN FRONT OF TOWN HALL THEN?

IMPOSSIBLE! THERE ARE TOO MANY PARKED CARS!

IN FACT, WE'D NEED TO FIND A PLACE PERFECTLY SUITED TO DANCING WHERE WE'D REALLY BE AT EASE...

!

I KNOW OF ONE!

ORGANIZING A FLASH MOB DANCE AT A DANCE SCHOOL IS ORIGINAL, ISN'T IT?

FOR SURE! NOBODY'S EVER THOUGHT OF THAT!

?

YOU'RE SICK, IT SEEMS, ALIA?

YES, I HAVE THE FLU!

THE FLU? IS THAT WHY YOU DIDN'T COME TO THE LAST DANCE CLASS?

THAT'S RIGHT! ≥SNIRFL≤

SINCE LUCIE AND JULIE TOLD US YOU HAD THE FLU, WE CAME BY TO SAY HI...

THAT'S NICE!

WE WERE NEARBY WITH BRUNO, SO WE CAME TO SEE IF YOU WERE DOING BETTER...

WE EVEN BROUGHT CARLA!

A FEW DAYS LATER...

AAAAH! I'M FINALLY BETTER! I CAN'T WAIT TO START DANCING AGAIN...

HELLO, GIRLS!

?!

SORRY, CLASS IS CANCELED. ALL THE STUDENTS CAUGHT THE FLU! I REALLY WONDER HOW, TOO...

SO, GIRLS, IT'S AGREED? WE'LL MEET ON WEDNESDAY AT 2PM AT THE ISIDORE PIRON PLAZA FOR A NEW FLASH MOB DANCE?

THAT WORKS!

WE'LL BE THERE!

ON WEDNESDAY...

BRUSH YOUR TEETH!

SORRY, I WON'T BE ABLE TO COME! I FORGOT ABOUT MY DENTIST APPOINTMENT!

NOT WITH US! OUR MATH TEACHER POPPED A QUIZ ON US FOR THURSDAY... YES, WE'RE STUDYING TOGETHER!

I'M STUCK, TOO! I HAVE TO BABYSIT CAPUCINE! LUCKILY, LUCIE'S WITH ME...

SINCE SOMETHING'S COME UP FOR EVERYONE, WE MIGHT AS WELL CANCEL...

YES, BUT WHAT'S ANNOYING IS THAT I CAN'T REACH ALIA!

Blip Blip Blip

SHE MUST HAVE ALREADY LEFT WITHOUT HER PHONE.

YOU'VE REACHED THE VOICEMAIL OF... ALIA...

THAT'S TOO BAD! BUT, SEEING US NOT COMING, SHE'LL SURELY FIGURE--

LET'S HOPE!

AT THE SAME MOMENT...

WELL, WHAT ARE THEY DOING?!

A FLASH MOB DANCE ALL BY YOURSELF ISN'T VERY FUN!

LINGERIE

COSTUME JEWELRY

ISIDORE PIRON PLAZA

JIM SAL

TODAY, WE'RE GOING TO REDO AN EXERCISE WE'VE ALREADY WORKED ON, BECAUSE IT'S VERY IMPORTANT.

IT'S ABOUT GETTING USED TO CONTINUING YOUR ROUTINE DESPITE WHATEVER'S GOING ON AROUND YOU!

SO I'LL TRY TO DO EVERYTHING I CAN TO DISTURB YOU, BUT NOTHING, ABSOLUTELY NOTHING MUST INTERRUPT YOU!

WHATEVER HAPPENS, YOU MUST *ALWAYS* KEEP ON DANCING! IS THAT UNDERSTOOD, GIRLS?

YES!

OKAY, MARY!

THEN, LET'S GO!

CLICK

A PIECE OF THE SET MIGHT BE LOCATED IN A BAD SPOT. IT'S UP TO YOU TO ADAPT!

!

A DANCER MAY GET A MOVEMENT WRONG...

...YOU HAVE TO GO ON WITHOUT LETTING YOURSELF BE THROWN OFF!

?!

AND EVEN A BRA STRAP THAT'S STARTING TO FALL MUSTN'T DISTRACT YOU!

!

MANY BOOBY-TRAPS LATER...

GOOD JOB, GIRLS, YOU'RE THE BEST! WE'LL STOP THERE!

click

??

HEY! YOU CAN STOP! WE'RE DONE!

!!

TWO HOURS LATER...

I PROMISE YOU, GIRLS, THE EXERCISE IS OVER...

I'D REALLY LIKE TO GO HOME NOW...

AND WHAT IF WE ALL BROUGHT AN ACCESSORY FOR OUR NEXT FLASH MOB DANCE?

LIKE-- I DON'T KNOW-- A HAT OR A SCARF.

WHY NOT SUNGLASSES? THAT'D BE VERY CLASSY.

OR THEN, WE COULD DANCE WITH AN UMBRELLA?

THAT'S A GOOD IDEA, CAMILLE, BUT THAT RISKS BEING A BIT CUMBERSOME. ....

IF YOU AGREE, LET'S GO WITH SUNGLASSES.

PERFECT!

⸲HEE HEE!⸴ IT'LL BE FUN!

THAT'S HOW IT GOES, GIRLS...

I'M SURE THAT IF WE'D CHOSEN THE UMBRELLA, IT WOULD HAVE BEEN SUNNY!

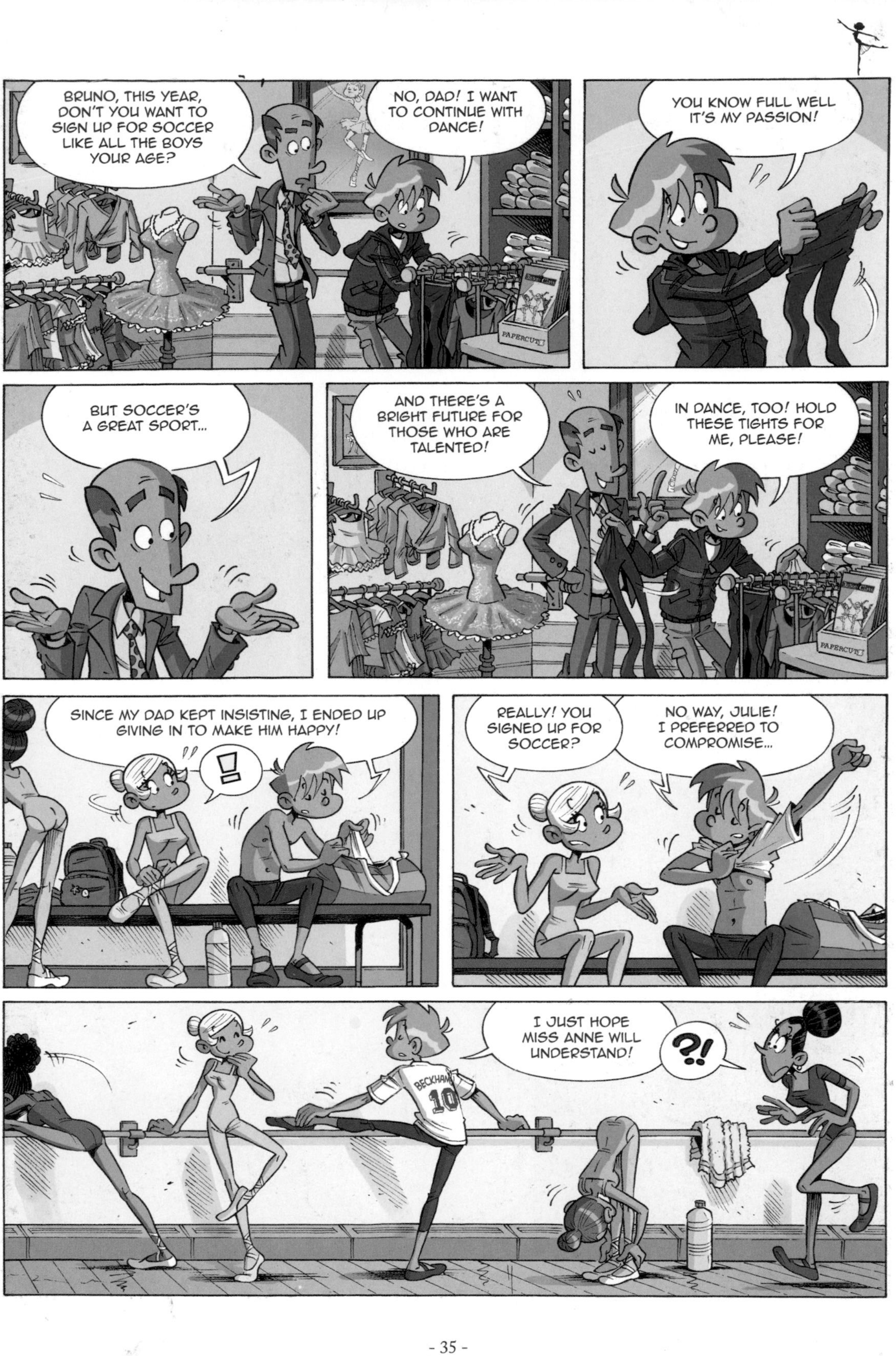
BRUNO, THIS YEAR, DON'T YOU WANT TO SIGN UP FOR SOCCER LIKE ALL THE BOYS YOUR AGE?
NO, DAD! I WANT TO CONTINUE WITH DANCE!
YOU KNOW FULL WELL IT'S MY PASSION!
PAPERCUT
BUT SOCCER'S A GREAT SPORT...
AND THERE'S A BRIGHT FUTURE FOR THOSE WHO ARE TALENTED!
IN DANCE, TOO! HOLD THESE TIGHTS FOR ME, PLEASE!
PAPERCUT
SINCE MY DAD KEPT INSISTING, I ENDED UP GIVING IN TO MAKE HIM HAPPY!
!
REALLY! YOU SIGNED UP FOR SOCCER?
NO WAY, JULIE! I PREFERRED TO COMPROMISE...
I JUST HOPE MISS ANNE WILL UNDERSTAND!
?!
BECKHAM
10

IT'S COOL THAT WE COULD THROW THIS PARTY AT YOUR PLACE, ALIA.

YEAH! YOUR PARENTS ARE REALLY NICE TO LET YOU USE THE APARTMENT!

OH, YOU KNOW, I REALLY HAD TO INSIST. BUT THEY ENDED UP AGREEING, SAYING THEY COULD TAKE THIS CHANCE TO GO OUT THEMSELVES.

TCHIKI TCHIKI BOOM

I THINK THEY MEANT TO GO SEE A CONCERT OR SOME-THING LIKE THAT.

TCHIKI BOOM

IN ANY CASE, THEY PROMISED ME THEY'D NOT COME BACK BEFORE MIDNIGHT! SO WE HAVE THE WHOLE TIME TO HAVE FUN, GIRLS!

TCHIKI BOOM

I HOPE YOUR PARENTS HAVE AS NICE AN EVENING AS US!

OH! I'M NOT WORRIED ABOUT THEM...

TCHIKI

TCHIKI BOOM

ON THE LANDING...

I'M TIRED OF BEING STUCK OUT HERE! YOU DON'T THINK WE COULD SNEAK BACK IN TO GET THE CAR KEYS?

NO! WE PROMISED! YOU SHOULDN'T HAVE FORGOTTEN THEM!

TCHIKI TCHIKI BOOM

TCHIKI TCHIKI BOOM!

ZZZZZ ZZZZZ

YOU WERE RIGHT, FRANK! THERE ARE PEOPLE SLEEPING ON OUR LANDING!

I'LL CALL THE POLICE!

TOWARDS MIDNIGHT...

THANKS, ALIA! YOUR PARTY WAS A BIG SUCCESS!

SEE YOU SOON, GIRLS!

THAT'S THAT, LEO! EVERYONE'S GONE!

SINCE MOM AND DAD HAVEN'T GOTTEN BACK YET, LET'S START STRAIGHTENING UP A BIT.

YOU KNOW, IT'S WEIRD THEY'VE STILL NOT GOTTEN BACK, ISN'T IT?

OH, YOU KNOW, THEY MIGHT AS WELL TAKE FULL ADVANTAGE OF GOING OUT FOR ONCE!

YOU WANT US TO BELIEVE THAT YOU LIVE THERE, BUT THAT YOU'D RATHER STAY IN THE HALLWAY...

...ALL TO LET YOUR KIDS HAVE FUN ON THEIR OWN?!

WOW! NOT A BAD ROUTINE, MARY!

VERY ORIGINAL!

WILL YOU TEACH IT TO US?

UH...

...IT'S MORE AN IMPROVISATION, YOU KNOW!

OH?

ON WHAT THEME?

THERE'S A WASP IN THE DANCE STUDIO!

BZZZ

BZZZ

BZZZ

! ! ! !!

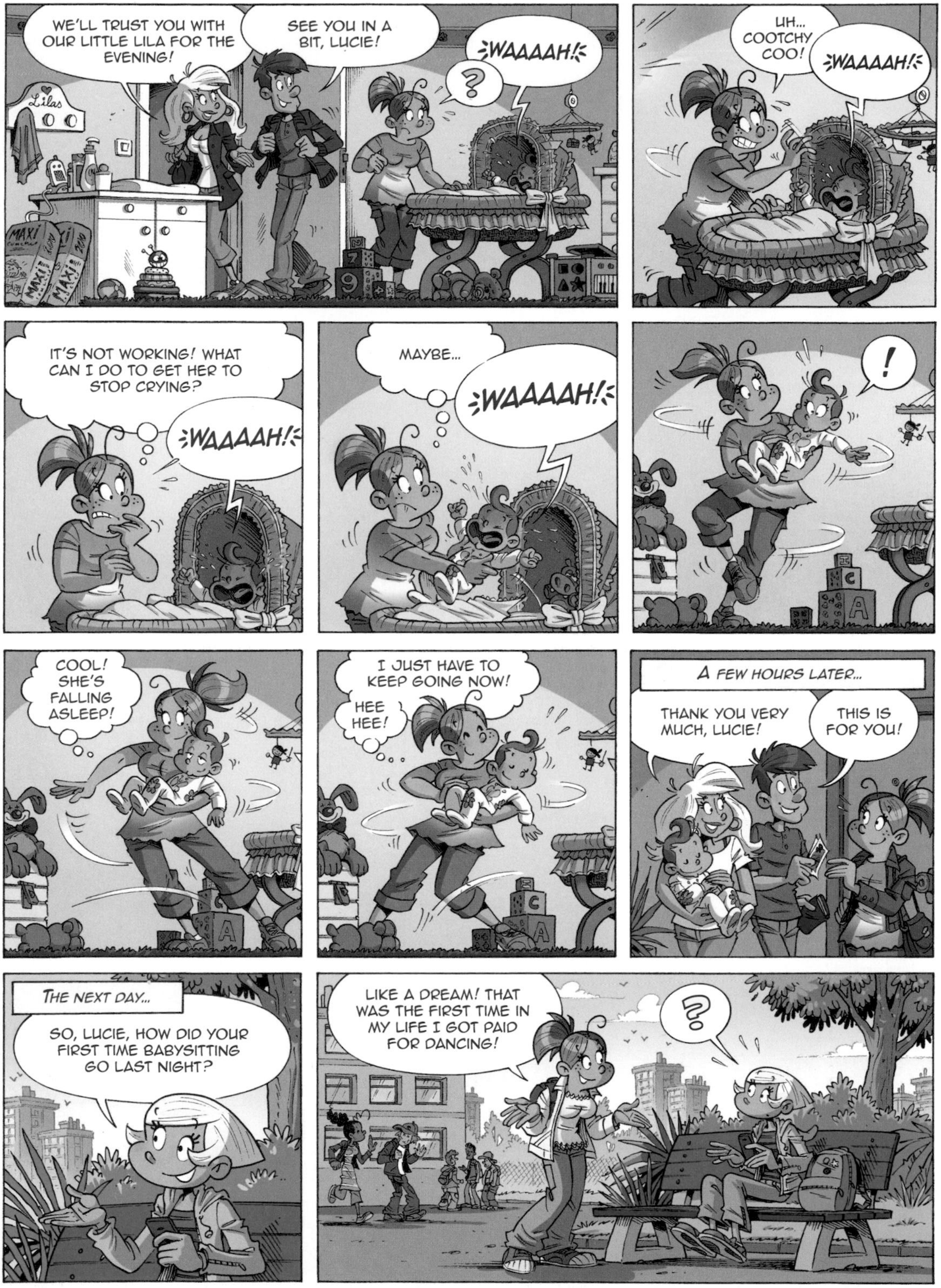
WE'LL TRUST YOU WITH OUR LITTLE LILA FOR THE EVENING!
SEE YOU IN A BIT, LUCIE!
Lilas
WAAAAH!
?
UH... COOTCHY COO!
WAAAAH!
IT'S NOT WORKING! WHAT CAN I DO TO GET HER TO STOP CRYING?
WAAAAH!
MAYBE...
WAAAAH!
!
COOL! SHE'S FALLING ASLEEP!
I JUST HAVE TO KEEP GOING NOW!
HEE HEE!
A FEW HOURS LATER...
THANK YOU VERY MUCH, LUCIE!
THIS IS FOR YOU!
THE NEXT DAY...
SO, LUCIE, HOW DID YOUR FIRST TIME BABYSITTING GO LAST NIGHT?
LIKE A DREAM! THAT WAS THE FIRST TIME IN MY LIFE I GOT PAID FOR DANCING!
?

...AND, TO FINISH, END WITH A *DEMI-PLIÉ EN COUPÉ ARRIÈRE!*

YOU MUST REMEMBER THIS ROUTINE BECAUSE, IN THE NEXT CLASS, I'LL ASK YOU TO PERFORM IT WITHOUT MISTAKES!

I'M COUNTING ON YOU TO REMEMBER IT.

YES, MISS ANNE!

GOOD-BYE!

IS SOMETHING WRONG, CAPUCINE?

I'M CONCENTRATING SO I WON'T FORGET MY ROUTINE FOR DANCE CLASS!

OH, I SEE!

AND SO...

UNTIL THE DAY OF THE DANCE CLASS...

HEE HEE! I REMEMBER IT PERFECTLY!

BUT AN HOUR LATER...

≥BOOHOO-HOO!≥

?

IT DIDN'T WORK, CAPUCINE? DID YOU MESS UP YOUR ROUTINE?

NO! ≥BOO-HOOOO!≥

BY THINKING ABOUT ONLY THAT, I FORGOT TO TAKE MY DANCE STUFF... AND I DIDN'T GET TO DANCE!

≥BOO-HOOO!≥

!

TODAY, WE'RE GOING TO WORK ON THE *PAS DE DEUX.*

AS ITS NAME INDICATES, IT'S A DANCE FOR TWO. SO CHOOSE A PARTNER AND--

!

BUMP

BUMP

AAAAAH!

BUMP

BUMP

BUMP

?

OUCH!

UH... OKAY!

WHILE BRUNO RECOVERS FROM THAT LITTLE INCIDENT, WE'LL WORK ON A FEW SOLO *ARABESQUES.*

HERE, LUCIE! SINCE YOU BABYSIT, I FOUND THIS AD IN THE HALL OF THE BUILDING WHERE I LIVE!

OH, THANKS, SAM! I'LL CALL RIGHT AWAY!

A FEW MOMENTS LATER...

SWEET! GIRLS, I'M STARTING TONIGHT!

WHAT'S MORE, IT PAYS REALLY WELL, SINCE IT SEEMS THE BABY HAS TROUBLE FALLING ASLEEP AND WAKES UP A LOT.

BUT THAT DOESN'T SCARE ME! I'VE SEEN OTHERS LIKE THAT...

GOOD LUCK, LUCIE!

I DON'T SEE WHAT THE PROBLEM IS! THIS BABY'S AS CUTE AS CAN BE, AND HE SLEEPS WELL.

BOOOM TABOOM BAM

?

!

BOOOM TABOOM BAM

WAAAH!

BOOOM TABOOM

BAM

REALLY NOW! WHO COULD BE MAKING SUCH A RACKET?!

SHHHHH! IT'S NOTHING! SHHHHHHH...

WAAAH!

I WONDER IF LUCIE GOT HIRED BY MY NEIGHBORS?

I'LL HAVE TO ASK HER TOMORROW.

BOOOM

TABOOM BAM

THAT'S STRANGE! ALL THE LITTLE GIRLS DANCE WITH THEIR HEADS TURNED TOWARDS THE SAME SIDE!

YES! AT THAT AGE, WE ALL DANCE LIKE THAT!

BUT I WON'T TELL YOU WHY, DAD! IT'S A DANCER'S SECRET!

LEG BACK IN A *DEMI-PLIÉ!* STRETCH THE OTHER ONE IN FRONT... VERY GOOD!

PERFECT! THE CHILDREN ARE MANAGING VERY WELL!

⇥WHEW!⇤ IT'S HOT IN THESE WINGS!

NOOOO! DON'T IMITATE ALL MY GESTURES!

NO! NO! STICK TO THE CHOREOGRAPHY!

STOOOOOOOP!

FORGET IT, ANNE, IT'S TOO LATE NOW! WE'LL JUST HAVE TO SAY IT WAS CONTEMPORARY DANCE!

WHAT ABOUT THOSE SHOES, JULIE?

THEY FEEL VERY GOOD ON ME, DAD!

BUT IT REMAINS TO BE SEEN IF THEY MAKE MY FEET PRETTY.

ONCE CAPUCINE HAS FINISHED PLAYING THE ADULT, YOU CAN GO LOOK AT YOURSELF IN THE MIRROR!

THERE'S NO USE, WAITING -- THERE'S SOMETHING SIMPLER!

AND HUP!

?!

YES, I THINK I'LL TAKE THEM!

!

YOU NEVER RUN OUT OF SURPRISES WHEN YOU HAVE A DAUGHTER WHO TAKES DANCE!

!

!

WATCH OUT FOR PAPERCUTZ™

Welcome to the sixth, snow-covered DANCE CLASS graphic novel by Crip & Béka. I'm Jim Salicrup, your Scrooge-like, social-dancing Editor-in-Chief of Papercutz, those energetic elves dedicated to publishing great graphic novels for all ages.

We've been receiving a lot of requests from you wanting to learn more about the creators of DANCE CLASS, and since we try to do everything we possibly can to please you, here's the secret story behind "Béka"...

Bertrand Escaich is one half of the writing team known as Béka. Bertrand was born in 1973 in Ariège, France. Because he could only find his favorite *Tintin* and *Asterix* comics in small local bookstores, he was soon compelled to begin writing and drawing his own comics. He later took his chances on sending a few stories to publishers that he drew himself, for lack of knowing any artists. Luckily, he was accepted by the publisher Vents d'Ouest as an artist. There, he made the acquaintance of Bloz, the future artist of *Fonctionnaires*, and of Poupard, the future artist of *Rugbymen*. In 2002, thanks to Bamboo Editions, he could finally devote himself to his true passion: writing humorous stories. In collaboration with Caroline Roque, he co-writes the gag series *Fourmidables*, *Footmaniacs*, and *Fonctionnaires*. They went on to create *the Rugbymen* and DANCE CLASS series.

Caroline Roque, the other half of the writing team known as Béka, was born in 1975 in Perpignan, France. She soon had her nose buried in books, first to color them, then to read them. Having studied chemistry to reassure her mom that she would find a good job one day, she decided instead to abandon her thesis and devote herself to writing comic-book scripts and novels. One of her stories received the prize for art house cinema in Toulouse, which encouraged her to continue in that direction. Around the time she abandoned her thesis, she met Bertrand and co-created *the Rugbymen* and DANCE CLASS graphic novel series with him.

That takes care of half of our DANCE CLASS creative team. As for "Crip," we hope to reveal that secret in an upcoming DANCE CLASS graphic novel. Possibly even in DANCE CLASS #7 "School Night Fever." So, there's yet another reason not to miss it!

Thanks,

Jim

STAY IN TOUCH!
EMAIL: salicrup@papercutz.com
WEB: www.papercutz.com
TWITTER: @papercutzgn
FACEBOOK: PAPERCUTZGRAPHICNOVELS
MAIL: Papercutz, 160 Broadway,
         Suite 700, East Wing, New York, NY 10038

More Great Graphic Novels from PAPERCUTZ™

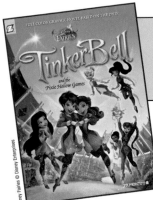

DISNEY FAIRIES #13
"Tinker Bell and
the Pixie Hollow Games"
Adapting the hit Tinker Bell
TV Special!

ERNEST & REBECCA #4
"The Land of Walking Stones"
A 6 ½ year old girl and her micro-
bial buddy against the world!

THE GARFIELD SHOW #2
"Unfair Weather"
As seen on the Cartoon Network!

Stardoll #1
"Secrets & Dreams"
Girls just want to have fun…
with fashion!

THE SMURFS #16
"The Aerosmurf"
It's a bird! It's a plane! It's a...
Smurf?

SYBIL THE BACKPACK
FAIRY #4
"Princess Nina"
Nina and Sybil's Excellent
Adventure Through Time!

Available at better booksellers everywhere!

Or order directly from us! DISNEY FAIRIES is available in paperback for $7.99, in hardcover for $11.99;
ERNEST & REBECCA is $11.99 in hardcover only; THE GARFIELD SHOW is available in paperback for $7.99, in hardcover for $11.99;
STARDOLL is available in paperback for $7.99 each, in hardcover for $11.99; THE SMURFS are available in paperback for $5.99, in
hardcover for $10.99; and SYBIL THE BACKPACK FAIRY is available in hardcover only for $10.99.

Please add $4.00 for postage and handling for the first book, add $1.00 for each additional book.

Please make check payable to NBM Publishing. Send to: PAPERCUTZ, 160 Broadway, Suite 700, East Wing, New York, NY 10038

(1-800-886-1223)